GW01395844

The Hospital

Mary O'Keeffe

GILL EDUCATION

Today we're going to learn a little bit about the hospital. Why might people be going in and out of the hospital?

When you see my red star beside a word, try to read it!

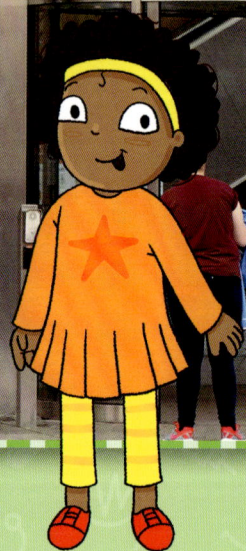

MATER HO

SPITAL

in

AMBULANCE

3

sit

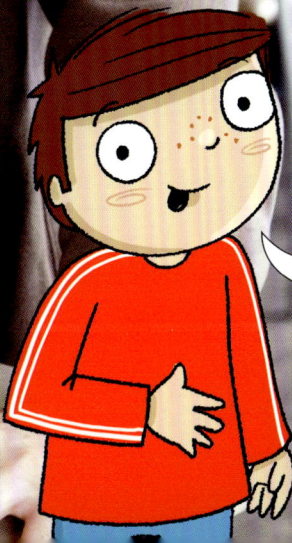

Pretend you are a patient. Can you give your personal details to the hospital receptionist?

Can you tell the story of how the doctor helps this little girl?

cut

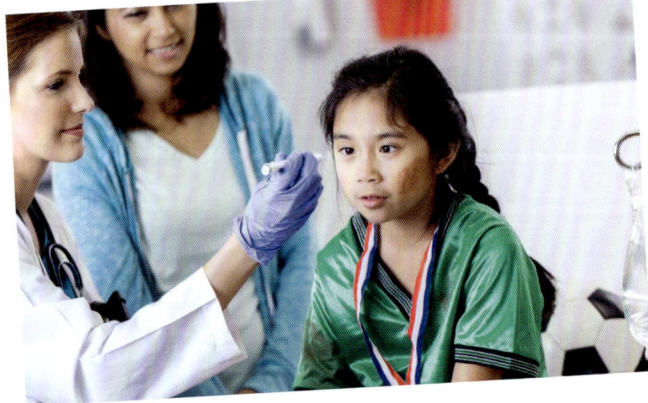

sad

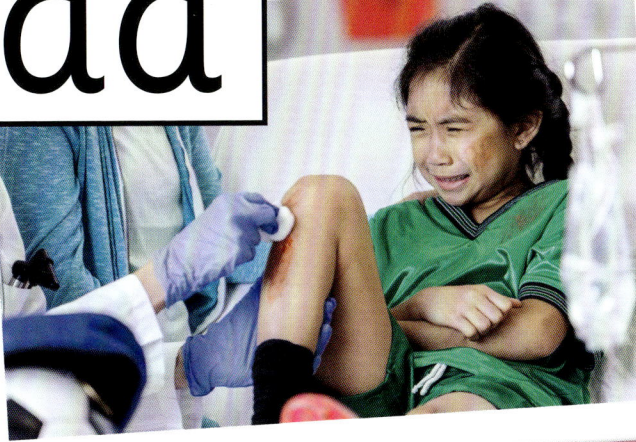

What is the nurse doing here?

pill

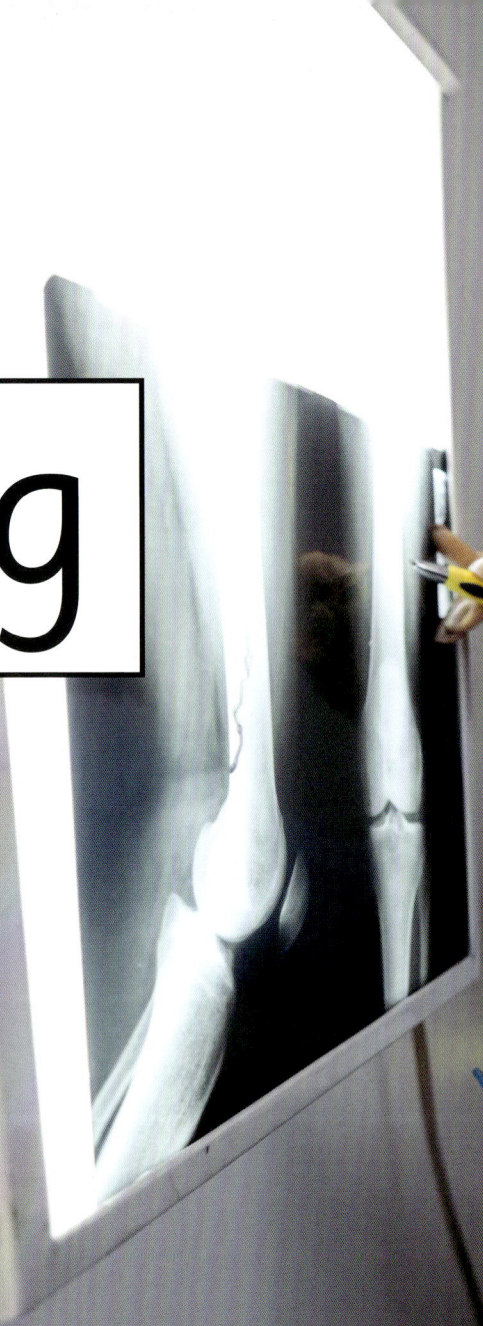

leg

Uh-oh! Can you see what's wrong with the patient's leg?

hat

Can you think why the surgeon might have to wear these special clothes?

bed

The little girl's leg is all better! Can you see what she has been using to help her walk while her leg heals?